D1401503

FOR LAUREN AND SISSY

A TALE FROM FLURRYVILLE

Arctic Bart Finds His Happy Heart

written and illustrated by
TODD LAMERTON

KENDALL/HUNT PUBLISHING COMPANY
4050 Westmark Drive   Dubuque, Iowa 52002

Arctic Bart was a quiet little snowman
who lived all by himself.

He lived *far* North of North in a magical wonderland
where anything was possible.

Most of Bart's days were spent dreaming
of a place where snowmen played together.

"If I left this place,"
he would sometimes say,
"I wonder if I
would find a friend?"

He imagined a big city,

a place where he knew he would not be alone.

But Bart *was* alone.

One day Bart looked outside his window, and to his surprise, he saw a small white dove sitting on a branch.

In the dove's beak was a note.

Bart read out loud,
"You have not because you ask not."

Then, as magically as he had appeared,
the dove flew away.

Arctic Bart wandered alone to the top of a distant hill.

"Oh please send me a friend!" he shouted.

That night the wind blew to and fro,
back and forth across the earth.

From the highest
mountains tiny flakes were
carried on the wind,

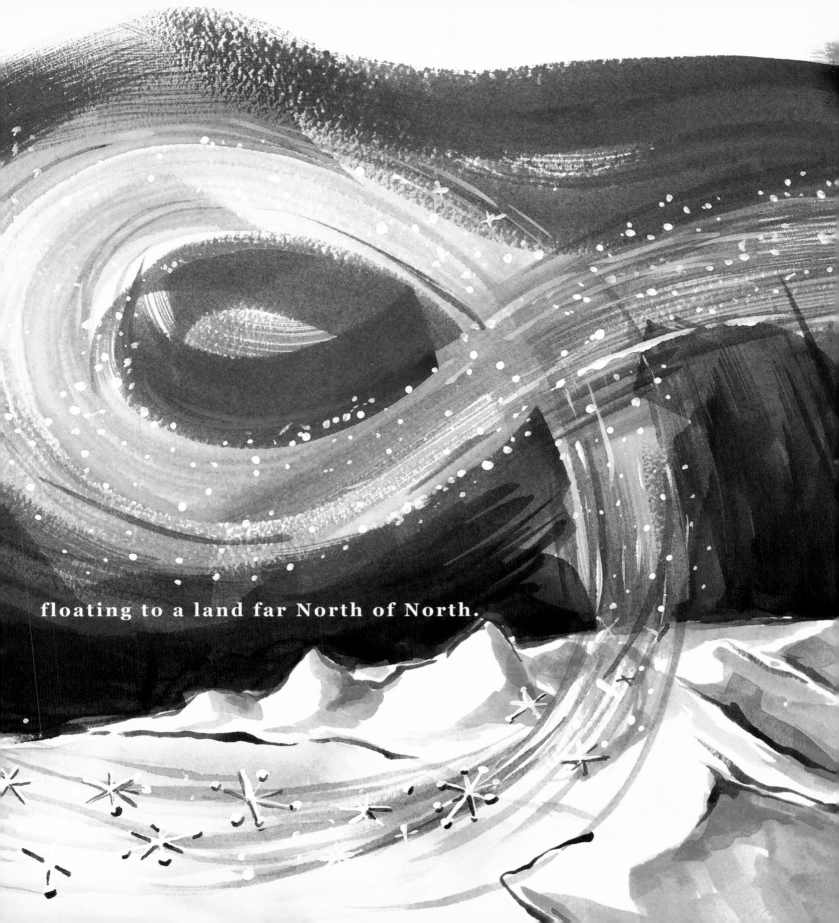

floating to a land far North of North.

Snowmen, snowmen, everywhere,
all hustling and bustling,
busy doing Snowman things!

"Let's get this banner finished so we can check the snowflake levels
and the blizzard report," Slushy Jo hollered to Shiverin' Dan.

"Welcome to Flurryville, Bart!

I'm Polar Paul, a loyal patriot of the

community," a snowman called out as he

waved his flag in the crisp morning air.

"Professor I. C. Winters at your service!
Bart, Flurryville has been a magical place since the first
Great Snow. It's a place where dreams come true."

"You have asked, you have believed, and now you have received."

"Oh, yes," added Crystal Claire,
"and to celebrate our Flurryville friendships,
we have a big celebration every year called

The Festival of Friends."

Flakey Jake, chairperson of
   the decorating committee,
was busy decking the town
   from top to bottom.

   More bows! More wreaths!
How beautiful our town will be!

Frosty Frank hauled in the tree that would soon
be placed at the center of the Festival.

"Thanks be to our good Friends of the Forest
who have given us such a lovely tree!"

With everything neatly in place,
the inhabitants of Flurryville gathered together
for the most exciting moment during the Festival.

Blizzard Bob climbed to the
top of a high ladder.

"With this star, I hereby declare
that the Festival of Friends can begin."

"Let's welcome Bart, our newest Flurryville friend!"

All the snowmen clapped and cheered. Snowdrift Sam played the old familiar tune that the snowmen sang every year since that first Great Snow.

All your dreams

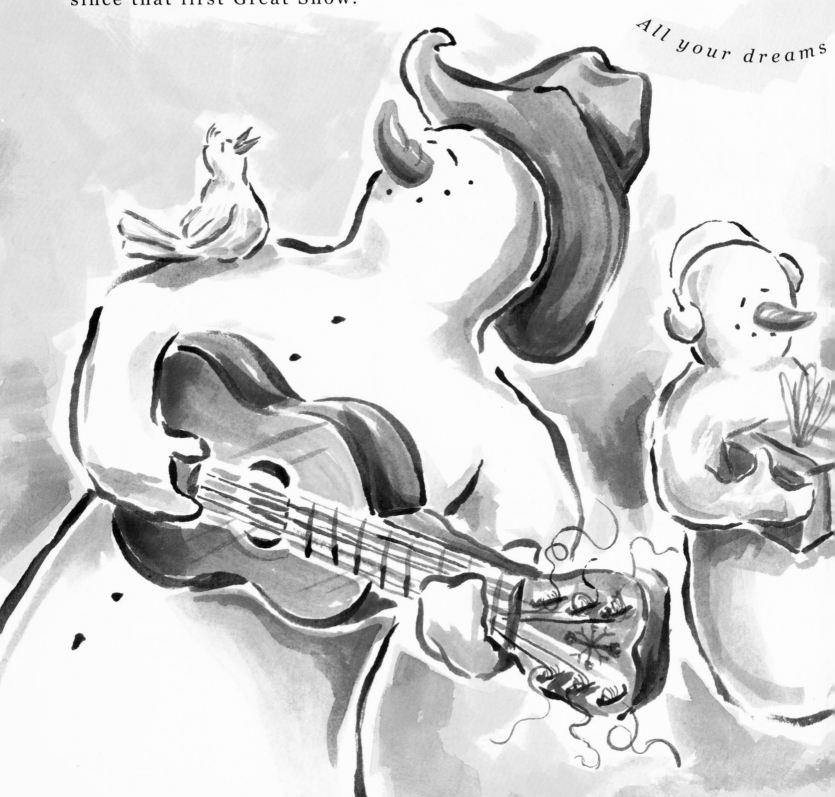

can be fulfilled when you dream of Flurryville...

And there, among his
new found friends, was
Arctic Bart and his happy heart.

THE END